Olof Krarer

Olof Krarer, the Esquimaux lady

A story of her native home

Olof Krarer

Olof Krarer, the Esquimaux lady
A story of her native home

ISBN/EAN: 9783337113186

Printed in Europe, USA, Canada, Australia, Japan

Cover: Foto ©Andreas Hilbeck / pixelio.de

More available books at **www.hansebooks.com**

OLOF KRARER

THE ESQUIMAUX LADY

A STORY OF HER NATIVE HOME

BY

ALBERT S. POST, A. M.

OTTAWA, ILLS.
1887

OLOF KRARER

THE ESQUIMAUX LADY

A STORY OF HER NATIVE HOME

BY

ALBERT S. POST, A. M.

OTTAWA, ILLS.
1887

Press of Wm. Osman & Sons.

INTRODUCTION.

IN writing this little book, it has been our constant aim to make it, as nearly as possible, an autobiography, giving Miss KRARER'S own thoughts and words, avoiding some of the little errors, caused by her imperfect knowledge of English, which are thought by some to add a certain charm to her conversation. If, near the conclusion, I may seem to have departed from this plan, it is only because she desired me to attempt the expression of her thought in more elaborate language than she can herself, at present, make use of.

She is authority for the facts, from beginning to end.

Hoping that the story of her eventful life may be as interesting to those who read, as it has already been to thousands who have heard it from her own lips; and with the heartfelt wish that it may be the means of enabling her to accomplish her cherished purpose, I am glad to have this opportunity of assisting in her work.

ALBERT S. POST.

OLOF KRARER.

I WAS born in Greenland, on the east coast. I am the youngest of eight children. My three sisters and four brothers are all living in Iceland. My father is living in Manitoba. My mother died in Iceland when I was sixteen years old.

We lived near the sea-shore in Greenland. Our house was built of snow. It was round, perhaps sixteen feet across, and coming to a point at the top. It was lined with fur on all sides, and was carpeted with a double thickness of fur.

The way they lined the house was to take a skin of some animal, and hold it near a fire, which was in the centre of the room. When the skin was heated through, they took it and pressed it against the wall. In a short time, it stuck to the wall so tightly that it could not be pulled off without tearing the skin.

The door was a thick curtain of fur, hung over the doorway, by heating the upper part, and letting it stick fast to the wall. Outside of the door was a long, narrow passageway, just high enough for one of us little Esquimaux people to stand up straight in. That would be about high enough for a child

six years old, in this country ; and it was only wide
enough for one person to go through at a time.   If
one wanted to go out, and another wanted to go in,
at the same time, one would have to back out and
let the other go first.   This passageway was not
straight ; but turned to one side, so as not to let the
wind blow in.

Our fireplace was in the centre of the house.   The
bottom was a large, flat stone, with other stones and
whalebone put about the edge to keep the fire from
getting out into the room.   When we wanted to
build a fire, we would put some whalebone and lean
meat on the stone; then a little dry moss was put
in, and then my father would take a flint and a
whale's tooth, or some other hard bone, and strike fire
upon the moss.   Sometimes he could do it easily,
but sometimes it took a long while.   After the fire
started he would put some blubber upon it.

Although it was so very cold, we would often be
without a fire, for what we made the fire of was what
we had to live on, and we could not always afford to
burn it.   Our fire did not warm the room very much.
It was mostly to give light, so that it might be a
little more cheerful in the room.   When we had no
fire it was very dark.

There was no chance to play round and romp inside the snow-house.   We just had to sit with our
arms folded and keep still.   It was in this way that
my arms came to have such a different shape from
people's arms in this country.   Where their muscle

is large and strong, I have but very little; and instead
of that, I have a large bunch of muscle on the upper
side of my arms, and they are crooked, so that I can
never straighten them. A doctor in Iceland once
tried to straighten one arm by pulling, but he could
not change it one bit; and it was very sore for a long
time afterward and the muscles were much swollen.
But it was not so with my father and brothers. They
went out to hunt and had more exercise and more
pulling to do, and so their arms were straight.

It was a great thing when the men would come
home from a hunt, for then we would have a great
deal to talk about:—how far they went, how cold it
was, how they found the bear, or walrus, or seal, and
who was most active and brave in killing it. Father
would often say to mother, "Oh, how I wish you had
been along, for we had such a nice drink of warm
blood." The warm blood of a dying animal was considered the greatest luxury we could get, because we
had not any cooked food at all. We ate it all frozen
and raw, except when fresh from the animal. It was
a great thing to strike the animal first with a spear,
for the one who drew first blood was owner of the
skin and was the boss of the whole job. They just
had to cut it to suit him. The flesh was divided
equally between all the hunters.

Sometimes we used to get very tired in the dark
snow-house, and then we would try a little amuse-
ment. Two of us would sit down on the fur carpet
and look into one another's faces and *guess who was*

the prettiest. We had to guess, for we had no looking-glass in which to see our own faces. The one whose face shone slickest with the grease was called the prettiest.

If at any time we grew too tired of it all and ventured to romp and play, we were in danger of being punished. As there were no trees from which to cut switches there, they took a different way. When any child was naughty, mother would take a bone and she would put it into the fire and leave it there until it was hot enough for the grease to boil out. Then she would take it and slap that on her child and burn it. She was not particular where she burned her child, only she was careful not to touch the face.

I can well remember what I got my last punishment for. I had been playing with my little brother inside the snow-house and I got mad at him, and so I threw him down and bit him on the back of the neck. Then mother heated a bone and burned me on the same place where I bit him. I got tired of that and didn't do that kind of a trick afterwards.

But it was not always so that we had to stay in the snow-house. Once in a while father would come in and say it was not so cold as usual, and then we would have a chance to look round outside the snow-house. We never took a long walk. As nearly as I can remember, my father's house was on a low plain near the sea-shore. It sloped gently inland, and we could have seen a great way into the back country if it had not been for the great snowdrifts and masses of ice. There were some steep, jagged rocks in sight of our village, and during the long daytime enough of the snow would melt off to leave the rocks bare in a few places. On these bare spots we would find a kind of brown moss, which we gathered and dried to light our fires with.

We never saw anything green in Greenland, and I never could understand why they called it by that name.

When we looked out toward the ocean, we could not see very far, for even in the warmest season there was only a small space of open water, and beyond that the ice was all piled up in rough, broken masses.

The great event in our family life, however, was the dog-sleigh ride. When father told us we could go, we came as near dancing and clapping our hands for joy as Esquimaux children ever did. But we did not have a fine cutter, with large horses and chiming bells. We did not even have an old-fashioned bob-sled, in which young men and young women have such good times in your country.

Sometimes the sleigh would be made of a great wide piece of bone from the jaws of a whale, one end of which turned up like a runner. But more often it would be either a skin of some animal laid flat on the ground, or a great frozen fish cut in two at the back and then turned right over. I never saw such a fish in this country, or in Iceland, so I cannot tell what kind of fish it was.

Our sleigh was drawn by dogs—sometimes six and sometimes ten or twelve. Each dog had a collar round his neck and a strip of reindeer hide tied into the collar and to the sleigh. When the dogs were well broken, they did not need any lines to guide them; but if they were not well trained, they had to have lines to control them. While we were getting ready to start, the dogs would jump about and whine and be as anxious to go as fiery horses in this country. The trained dogs would run forward and put their noses right into their collars without any trouble. When all was ready, away we went! It was great fun! The dogs could carry the sleigh faster than horses do in this country. Sometimes the sleigh was bumped and tumbled about a good deal on the rough ice, and once in a while it tipped over.

The dogs are about the size of shepherd dogs and have sharp pointed ears. They are very strong, and have heavy coats of long hair, which often drags upon the snow. They are of a dirty gray color.

When my father had as many as ten or twelve dogs, he had a separate snow-house for them and kept them in that; but when he had lost or lent his dogs, so that he had only two or three, he would let them come into the snow-house with us. Our dogs had the same kind of food to live on that we had, and sometimes when food was scarce they had a hard time of it. They were never fed when we were going to start out for a sleigh ride, for then they would lie right down and refuse to move one step.

But whenever we came back from a ride they were well fed.

Our dogs were very useful to us in other ways than drawing our sleighs, for they were very sharp and good to hunt. They helped to kill the polar bear, and to find the seal and walrus.

Now, in order that you may understand our way of living better, I will explain that we have six months' night in Greenland, and during that time nothing is seen of the sun. The moon changes very much as it does here, and we have the light of the stars. Then most of the time the beautiful northern lights may be seen dancing and leaping about, with many colored rainbow beauties. The white snow is always on the ground, so that even when the moon and northern lights did not show, we could see to hunt round. Before and after the night time, there was about a month of twilight, and this was our finest time of the year. We had then the best chance to hunt.

In the long day we had the hardest time, for then the sun shone out so brightly that we would be made snow blind if we ventured far from home. The day was four months long, and if we did not have food enough stored away in an ice cave to last us through, we would be in great danger of starving.

The best time to hunt is when the ice breaks up. My people know when this is going to happen by the noise. There is a rumbling sound like distant thunder. Whoever hears that sound first goes from house to house and gives warning, so that all may be ready to join in the hunt. Then the hunters get their spears and let out their dogs, and hurry to the place where the sound is heard. The polar bear hears the sound also, and hastens to the place, for it is here that he, too, must make his living. This is the only time that Esquimaux ever dare to tackle a polar bear, for when he is going about alone and hungry he is very fierce and dangerous; but when the ice breaks up the bear goes straight for the sound. This grows louder and longer, until there is a mighty crash, louder than thunder, and great walls of ice are thrown high in air, and a space of open water is to be seen. When the commotion has ceased, my people crowd along the edge of the water. They first look out for the bear, for they don't want him to catch any of their seals. They have some of their dogs loose in front of the sleigh, and some of them harnessed to it. When they come to the bear, he is busy watching for seal and pays very little attention to the hunters or their dogs. The loose dogs run up to him and begin to worry him. He chases some of them, and the others bite him behind. If he makes a rush at the hunters in their sleighs, the dog teams draw them swiftly away. The loose dogs keep on worrying the bear until he becomes furious with rage. Every little while a sweep of his huge paw lays one of his enemies on the snow, silent in death. A few minutes later, perhaps, another will be caught up in the powerful embrace of the great brute. The dogs crowd in and take hold wherever they can. The bear grows frantic in his struggles to punish his adversaries. At last he lies at full length panting upon the snow. Then it is that some hunter ventures to leave his dog-sled and try to kill him with a walrus tusk. No sooner is he sure that the animal is dying than he hastens to get a drink of warm blood. Then a long cut is made down the belly of the animal with the points of the walrus tusks and the skin is pulled and pushed off with their hands. All hands feast upon the warm grease that is inside the animal, and after that they divide the meat and take it home.

I will now explain that the breaking up of the ice I have told about is not from thawing. In the warmest time we ever saw in that part of Green-land where I came from, it never thawed enough to make the water run in streams. A few bare spots were melted off on the rocks and high points of land. Once in a while the snow would melt enough to drip a little, and form icicles, but not often. It was cold, cold, bitter cold, all the year round, and the people in this country can hardly have an idea of it, even in the coldest weather here. From this we see that there could be no chance for heat enough to make the thick ice break up by thawing. Have you ever seen a tub which was full of water frozen nearly solid? Then, perhaps you remember that the middle was heaved up and cracked to pieces by the frost. This, I think, is what takes place in the Northern seas, only on a far grander scale. A rumbling sound can be heard for some time before it really breaks up; but when it does come, there is an awful roar like loudest thunder, and great blocks of ice are lifted and piled one above another, until they are higher than the tops of the highest buildings in this country. As it breaks up a good many times in the same place, these ice mountains are piled higher and higher, until they get so large we cannot see over them or round them at all. Each time the ice breaks up, there is an open space where the water is free from ice, and the walruses and seals come up to breathe. Sometimes a walrus will crawl away from this opening far enough for the hunters to head him off and kill him. The walrus is hard to kill, for he is so watchful, and there is no way to call him as they do the seal. But when killed he is quite a prize.

In hunting the seal, they take a different plan. The seal is very fond of its young. The hunters will take advantage of this by lying flat on the ice and making a sound like the cry of a young seal. In this way they manage to call the old seal out on the ice. But even then it is not always easy to catch the seal, for it has a strong, flexible tail, by means of which it is able to throw itself a good many feet at a time, so that even when on the ice it sometimes gets away with its awkward rolls and flops and jumps. A seal is very active and almost always in motion.

Our greatest prize was the whale. Once in a while

one would get entangled in the breaking ice so that
it could not get away, and then everybody would be
out to help or see the fun. A great many ropes of
reindeer hide would be brought out and a great
many spears stuck into the animal. Then the men
would join together and try to pull the huge creature
out of the water. Even with the help of all the dogs
that could be used it was hard work, but they would
manage it after a while. Then all would give a great
shout and have great joy over the whale. One reason
for their rejoicing was that the whale had so much
blubber. Blubber is the inside fat of the whale.
There is a fine skin over it and it looks like tallow
or leaf lard. It is quite hard in my country, but
would melt down into what you would call whale oil
in this country. After the whale is cut up we would
have a great feast and eat all we could. Then, after
taking the meat home, we would spend a long time
eating and sleeping.

It was only when the ice broke up and the people
came together to hunt that they met one another.
All the rest of the time the families stay in their
own homes, and do not visit back and forth as your
people do. The only exceptions are, when a man
needs meat, or blubber, or a flint, and goes to borrow,
or when a young man goes to steal his girl. There
is no buying and selling, and no trading. Any one
can get what he needs by asking for it, if it is in the
village. The people try to treat each other as brothers and sisters.

I will now explain a strange custom among our people. When a young man gets to be about 25 years old he is full grown and is considered to be of age. He then begins to think of beginning life for himself. It is a risky thing in my country to get a wife. A young man has to steal his girl out of her parents' snow-house and get her away into another. If he is caught trying to do this the girl's parents turn right on him and kill him. If he has not pluck enough to steal a girl for himself, he has to live alone, and when he goes to sleep he crawls head first into a fur sack. When he wants to get up he must crawl out backwards. I suppose he is what you would call an old bachelor.

A young man, who sees a girl he thinks he would like to have for a wife, makes a great many excuses to come to her father's snow-house. Sometimes he wants to borrow a flint, or blubber, or something else. If he comes without any excuse, the girl's parents tell him, " I know very well what you do want; you want my girl, but you never shall get her." Then he gets kind of scared and runs off. But he sneaks round again pretty often. He thinks may be her parents will go out for a dog-sleigh ride, or may be they would lay them down to sleep some time. If he does get her out of the snow-house without being caught, the girl's parents send right back for him and think nobody is any smarter than he is, and do all they can for him.

The reason a girl's parents want the young man

to steal her is, that they want to find out whether he is willing to risk his life for his own girl or not. They think if he is not smart enough to steal a girl, he would not be smart enough to take care of her— kill a polar bear, so that she would have enough to live on.

There are not many old bachelors in my country, for if a man has not spunk enough to steal a girl he is looked down upon as a sort of soft, good-for-nothing fellow.

Many people are disappointed when they see me, because I am not darker colored, with black hair. More of my people have light hair than dark, and we know that we are naturally a fair-skinned people, because when a baby is born in my country it is just as white as any American baby, and it has light hair and blue eyes. But the mother does not wash it with soft water and soap, as they do in this country, but she goes to work and greases it all over, and the child is never washed from the day he is born till he dies, if he remains in that country. The mother wraps her little one in the skin of a young seal, which has been made very soft by pounding and rubbing it on the ice. If baby cries, the mother will not take it up and care for it, but she puts it in a corner and leaves it there until it stops crying, and then she takes it up and pets it. She can only nurse it about a month. Then the mother will warm some blubber for it; but in a little while it must live just like the rest. She carries the baby in her hood, and does not expect it to learn to walk until between two and three years old. Then she makes a suit for it of young seal's fur. When the child becomes larger, say six or seven years old, a thicker suit is made of polar bear skin; and then little "Auska" feels as proud of his new clothes as "Our Charlie" does of his new boots, and the chubby "Roegnia" rejoices over her white suit as much as dainty Flora in her arctics and muff and fur collar. But Auska and Roegnia are dressed more nearly alike than Charlie and Flora. Men's clothes are just like women's clothes; only a woman's coat comes down to a point and man's coat is cut off square, and that is all the difference. They wear fur mittens and fur shoes.

I think it would be very nice for some ladies in this country, if they were to go to Greenland; for they would have no washing, no ironing, no scrubbing and no cooking to do. They don't even have to wash their faces or comb their hair. Esquimaux people have only the salt ocean water, and if they had soft, fresh water they dare not use it, for it would be like poison to their flesh when the thermometer was 60° or 70° below zero. So, when they eat, my people take a chunk of raw meat in one hand and a chunk of blubber in the other, and take a bite of each until it is eaten. Then they carefully rub the grease and fat all over their hands and face, and feel splendid afterwards.

The women have long hair, made dark by the

smoke and grease. The men have long hair, also, and a thin, scattering beard over the face, which they never shave or trim, because they have no razor or shears.

We had no church or court house, no school or factory, no doctor, lawyer or merchant, no money, jewelry or timepiece, not an axe, spade or hammer, no knife, fork or spoon, no bread, no cloth, no wood! I never saw as much wood in my country as would make one little match. For a needle we use the tooth of a fish; for thread the sinews of a reindeer.

Rich people were those who had a flint. Poor people had to go and borrow it when they wanted to light a fire. Common folks would sit down flat on the fur carpet, but "tony" people would get blocks of ice or snow and put in the snow-house and cover them with fur for seats. But it was only the *most toniest* people who did that kind of a trick.

My people believe in good and bad spirits. They think there is a big Good Spirit and several small ones, and one big bad spirit and several small ones. They think if they tell a lie or do anything wrong, the bad spirit will come and hurt them some way. If a baby gets sick the mother does not do anything for it. She thinks a bad spirit has hold of her child, and will get her too if she helps it in any way. If baby dies she lays it away in the cold snow and leaves it without a tear. When a man is sick they carry him into a separate snow-house, and all they do to help him is to throw in a piece of poor meat which they do not care about themselves. If a woman is sick she is not taken from her snow-house, but is no better cared for. The only disease is something like consumption in this country. After an Esquimaux dies they drag him out and bury him in the snow, piling blocks of ice as high as they can above the grave. If he has not specially given his spear and flint and skins to some of his friends before he dies, then everything is buried with him, and the friends go home to think no more about him. If the white bear comes along and digs up the body they do not care. They never speak of a departed friend, because they fancy it would annoy the spirit, which is supposed to be not far off.

When a man is first taken sick they do one thing for him, if he is not very bad. They gather round him and sing to the Good Spirit, in hopes that He will drive away the bad spirit. If the sick man recovers they think a great deal of him.

Sometimes my father would tell us stories about his parents and grand parents, and then he would tell how they said that their parents told how long, long ago the first people had come from Norway. But no one knew what Norway was like. Some said it was a great house somewhere; some said it was the moon, and some said it was where the Good Spirit lived.

One thing had a great deal of interest for us all. When the sun shone out brightly at the beginning of the daytime it marked the first of the year, just as New Year's Day in this country. Then mother and father would bring out the sacks. Each one was made of a different kind of fur. Father had his, mother had hers, and each of the children one. In each sack was a piece of bone for every first time that person had seen the sun. When ten bones were gathered they would tie them into a bundle, for they had not words to count more than ten.

In such a land was I born. In such a home was I brought up. In such pleasures I rejoiced, until there were about fourteen bones in my sack. Then something happened which changed my whole life. Six tall men came to our village. Our men were much frightened at first and did not know what to make of the giants. Some thought them bad spirits. But they were peaceable, and went hunting with our people and helped them, so that after a while they came to like one another. The strangers were Iceland fishermen. After they lived with us for more than a year, they were able to explain how they were shipwrecked in a storm, and how they got on the ice and walked on the ice till they came to Greenland. They told/how much they wanted to get back to their families, and how much better country Iceland was. At last, three Esquimaux families told the Icelanders they would lend them their dogs and sleds if they would do them any good. And because they wanted their dogs back again they said they would go with them.

So they started out. My father's family was the largest in the party, there being ten of us in all. Most Esquimaux families had only three or four children in them—sometimes only one child, and often none at all. I was a young and giddy thing then, and was glad to go. We traveled a long way down the coast, hunting as we went. Then we turned right out on to the ocean itself. On the way there were three polar bears killed and some seals and other animals, so that we had plenty to eat. I remember we would sometimes take something to eat when the sledges were flying over the ice with the dogs at full gallop. At intervals we fed the dogs, and they gathered closely round the sled and soon all were asleep. When we woke up we went on again. While on the ocean we often heard the sound of the ice breaking up, and would have to hurry away to escape being caught in the upheaval. We finally reached Iceland after being two months and some days on the way, according to the Icelanders' calculation, and having traveled about a thousand miles.

The people in Iceland were astonished to see us little people. They came to see us from a long distance. We were all weighed and measured. My father stood three feet five inches, and weighed 160 pounds. My mother was the same height woman that I am, and weighed 150. None of my brothers was quite so tall as my father, but they came near his weight. One of my sisters was only three feet two inches, and weighed 142. I weighed 136 pounds.

Now I am three feet four inches high, and weigh 120.

The missionaries in Iceland took great interest in us, for they knew we were all heathens, and they said they would like to take us into their schools and educate us. So each family was taken into a different school. Our family was placed in the Lutheran school, and there I studied for five years. My teacher was a good and kind man. His name was Ion Thorderson. He was patient with me and helped me to learn; but some of the scholars were jealous of " the little thing" and made fun of me. For this they had to carry notes home to their parents, and this secured to them a good whipping a-piece, so that they were heard to wish "that little thing" had never come into the school.

At first we lived several miles from the school, but we did not know anything about walking, in fact could not walk any distance, so they sent us on horseback. They used to tie me on so that I would not fall off. It was a funny sight to behold us eight little tots going to school.

I never shall forget the time when a kind friend gave me a pony. He was very gentle, and small enough so that by leading him along side a large stone I was able to climb upon his back. He would stand quietly and wait for me. I loved my pony and thought there was nothing in the world like him. But this long ride was very hard on us, and finally the teacher made arrangement so that we could live close to the school.

The school system was very different in some respects from American schools. The teacher was always the minister, and the school was connected with the church. A scholar had first to learn to read, and must keep at it until he could read better than the teacher. Then he was called upon to commit to memory large portions of history and of the Bible; and when he had learned them so well that he could repeat from beginning to end without the book, he was allowed to begin to write. He could not take pen in hand before that. After learning to write, he was taught figures; and after that I do not know what was done.

The teacher never laid a hand on the scholar in punishment. If he did anything wrong, a note was sent to his parents, and they flogged him soundly.

I enjoyed the life in Iceland, for I saw and learned so much that was new.

Some time in the spring there was a holiday, in which the young folks would cut up pranks, something like the tricks of April-fool Day here. The girls would try to fasten a small sack of ashes upon the clothing of the boys, and they, in return, would seek to place a pebble in the pockets of the girls, endeavoring to do it so slyly that the sack or pebble would be carried about all day without the one who bore it knowing anything about it.

On one of these days, a girl tied a small sack into the beard of one of the men, while he was asleep, and he wore it all day before anyone told him, and then they had a great laugh at his expense. I thought I would try my hand at this, so I made a little sack and tucked it into the corner of a patch, which a big fellow wore upon his pants, the corner being ripped just enough to let the sack slip inside. I had great fun watching him all day, and when night came, he boasted that none of the girls had fooled him that day. "Oh, yes," said one of his companions, "the smallest girl in the house has fooled you badly." He felt pretty cheap when I pointed to the patch, and he found the sack sticking out so that he might have seen it easily.

Picking up fuel was hard work, and took a great deal of time. They had but little wood, and no coal, so that it was necessary to gather the droppings of animals, and make great piles of this kind of stuff in the summer, so that it would be dry enough to burn in the winter.

If mice came about the houses and buildings in the fall, the Icelanders would fear a hard winter, and much damage to their sheep; for when the winter grew very severe, and the mice could get nothing else to eat, they would climb upon the sheep's backs, while they were lying close together in the sheds, and would burrow into the wool, back of the shoulder-blades, and eat the flesh, very often causing the death of the poor animals.

The Icelanders used sheep's milk a great deal, and I liked it. Sheep's milk is richer and sweeter than cow's milk. They used to put up a lot of milk in

barrels, and put in some rennet, which would make
it curdle into something like cottage cheese. This
they would set aside for winter use, and all were
very fond of it. The family would be considered
very poor who could not put up from eight to ten
barrels of this food.

They sometimes, also, would churn mutton tallow,
or whale oil, in the sheep's milk, and make a kind of
butter. Whale oil makes a better butter than the
tallow, and I think I like would it even yet.

While most people had dishes and knives and
forks, it was not customary to set the table, unless
there was company present. Each one had a cup
for himself, made of wood with staves like a barrel,
and curiously bound with whale-bone hoops. They
had handles upon them, but I do not know how fast-
ened. A child's cup would hold about a quart, and
a man's cup sometimes as much as three quarts.
When each one had gotten his cup filled, he would
take his place at any convenient spot in the room,
on the bed, or anywhere, and proceed to empty the
cup with great haste. We all had ravenous appe-
tites, but did not always have enough to eat. In
the spring we had a great treat, when the eggs and
flesh of wild fowl were to be had. We fared well
when fish were plenty, but at other times a porridge
made of Iceland moss and the curdled milk made up
our fare. Some seasons they can raise a few vege-
tables in Iceland, but this is not often. Of late years
they cannot raise grain, although they used to raise
good oats.

One of the books that we had there was a history of America, and in that it said that money could be picked up off the streets, almost. I have since found it quite a difficulty. But that book put me into the notion to come out here. So when a colony of five hundred Icelanders were about to start for Manitoba, I got my father to come with them. He had just money enough to bring himself and one of his children, so he naturally chose his youngest and the one that was most anxious to come.

My mother died with consumption when we had been in Iceland about a year. I shall never forget the circumstances of her illness. I hated her, and turned from her just as we did in Greenland. She thought it was all right, and told me to keep away and to hate her, for fear the bad spirit would get me.

I said to my teacher one day: " I hate my mother." "Why, my dear child, you should not do that."

" But I do hate her; she has a bad spirit in her, and Esquimaux people always hate their friends when they get bad spirits in them."

Tears ran down the good man's cheeks as he exclaimed, " Why, the dear child, she doesn't know anything !"

Then he took me upon his knee and began to explain that my mother did not have a bad spirit, but was sick. He dropped his school work entirely, and for three days devoted himself to explaining the Christian belief. Then he made me go to my mother and tell her all about it. My mother was glad—oh, so glad; and she died happy.

My four brothers and three sisters are in Iceland, yet. I promised when I left that I would send for them, and I still hope to have them all with me.

We sailed in a ship from Iceland to Scotland. I cannot remember at what city we landed. From there I had my first railway ride, into England, and was much frightened by the noise and motion of the cars. Then we sailed to Quebec, and then came to Winnipeg. It took us five months and five days to come from Iceland to Manitoba.

When I came to Manitoba, I was sick for nearly two years. The Iceland ministers were very kind to me, and took care of me while I was sick. When I got well, I started out to work for my living. I could not speak one word of English, and I was afraid to try.

The first person I worked for was a half-breed woman, who had a rough, quarrelsome lot of children that I had to wait upon. Once in a while I was called into the front room, and would find some strangers there. One day the mistress was called away, when I was sent into the room, and the gentleman and lady who were there gave me a quarter, each. She had been making money out of me in this way all the while, but all the money I received for some months of hard labor was what these people gave me.

Then I was taken sick with the measles. The woman turned me out of doors. I did not know where to go. . I just ran round and round the house.

A young lady, from one of the best families in Winnipeg, found me in this plight, took me by the hand and led me home. She nursed me till I was well, and then gave me good clothes and found me a place to work. She told me to come back to her if I was in trouble again.

After working for some time in this place, I came to work for Mrs. C., the lady who is with me now. When she first saw me she thought I was a little child, and did not see how I could be of any use to her. But she pitied me because she thought I was cold, and gave me something to do. I lived with her three months. When I first came to her I could not speak enough English to tell her I liked coffee better than tea. My work was washing dishes. They would help me into a chair so that I could reach the table. When at last I was able to explain, with the help of an Iceland girl who lived next door, that I desired to travel as a curiosity, hoping in this way to make money enough to bring my brothers and sisters from Iceland, Mr. and Mrs. C. consented to come with me.

My father agreed to let me go, if I would go with respectable people and remain with them. I had worn my seal skin suit about in Manitoba until it was worn out, but my father had taken care of my polar bear suit, so I had that to bring with me. He let me bring his new flint and walrus tusk, also.

But a few months afterwards he sent for his spear, because he thought he could not get along without it, so I returned it to him. He is still living in Manitoba, and is 65 years old. This is several years older than people live in Greenland. Oldest people we ever knew were 60 years old. This I know from the Icelanders, who went round to all the snow houses and counted the bones in the different sacks.

When I reached Minneapolis I was taken sick, and the doctors did not know what to do for me. They kept me in a warm room, and I grew worse every day. At last Mr. C. heard of a doctor who had been in Greenland, and sent for him. Under his advice I was taken to Minnetonka and kept in a cold room, and I got well.

At first I traveled as a curiosity and charged ten cents. All I could do was to let the people see me, show my costume, flint and tusk, sing a few songs, etc. By degrees I learned to answer questions, and at last came to talk pretty well. While we were at a place in Indiana, called Cloverdale, some professors and a minister urged me to give a lecture. They secured a large hall, and when I peeked through a hole in the curtain I saw about 300 people, and was nearly scared out of my wits. But Mrs. C. got me mad over something about my dress, and the curtain went up while I was standing there, and I spoke to them right along. That was Dec. 30th, 1884. Since then I have been lecturing right along, except in some short times of sickness, and the hottest weather. I have been in Minnesota, Wisconsin, Iowa, Ilinois, Michigan, Ohio, Indiana, Missouri, Kansas, and Nebraska, and I hope by next year, to have all my brothers and sisters with me, so that we can travel together and help the missionary teachers in Iceland, where we got our education in the first place.

A great many funny things have been said to me by visitors, and a great many curious questions asked. Generally, people are kind and considerate, but sometimes they are rude and uncivil. I am always glad to satisfy reasonable curiosity to the best of my ability, but I do not like impertinence any better than any body else.

I was somewhat surprised by one old lady, a year or so ago. After she had listened for some time, and become greatly interested, she came up and said, "Where did yeou say yeou kum from?" "From the eastern coast of Greenland." "Greenland! why la, yes. I know that country. My husband's got a farm there." A farm in Greenland! Well, a good many other people have made mistakes fully equal to the old lady's.

Americans, I think you do not realize your blessings in this great land of plenty, where you have so many fine things. Even here, I often see sad faces, and hear words of discontent. Sometimes I am a little discontented myself, when I see something I want, and think I cannot, or ought not to, have it. But I soon get over that feeling when I remember my home in the frozen north, where we sat still through the weary hours, shivering with the cold, choked by the smoke, and often almost perishing with hunger.

If I was to go back to my race of people, I would
not be able to tell them about what I see and hear
in this country. They have not the language to
express the thought. They have seen nothing like
a sewing machine, or a piano. They have no mate-
rials to enable them to make machines. They never
saw a painting or a drawing. Their wild, rude songs
is all they have that is anything like music. They
have no idea of a book. They eat when they're
hungry, and sleep when they're sleepy. They are
happy and contented *when they don't know any better.*

The only relatives we knew about, were brothers
and sisters, father and mother, and our grandparents.
As for other relatives, such as uncles, aunts and
cousins, we knew nothing about them. We lived in
small settlements of thirty or forty families. No one
seemed to take any interest in finding out how many
settlements there were, or how many people lived in
them. We had only one name each, just as you
name animals in this country. My father's name
was Krauker. My name was Olwar. Before we left
Iceland, the whole family were baptized. They
named my father Salve Krarer, and they baptized
me Olof Krarer, making the Iceland names as near
like the Esquimaux names as they could, but giving
my father a new name, Salve, which means something like "saved."

THE END.

EPITOME.

On Iceland's damp and stormy shore,
Mid Geyser's throe and Ocean's roar,
A sturdy race on sterile soil,
Pursue their unremitting toil;
Struggling against stern poverty,
And Denmark's hostile mastery.
Farther northward, bleak and cold,
Bound by Winter's icy hold,
Where eternal snows abound,—
There the Esquimaux is found.
House of ice and suit of fur;
Food, the flesh of polar bear;
Tusks of walrus, the only arm,
Ferocious beasts alone alarm;
A dog-sleigh ride his only pleasure;
A piece of flint his choicest treasure;
Ambition's height to steal a wife,
For her he dares to risk his life.
He tells no lie nor ever swears;
For neighbor, as for brother, cares.
The golden rule he never heard,
But tries to keep its every word.
Father to son the story told,
How sailors hardy, brave and bold,
Far back in bygone centuries,
Sought to explore the Northern seas;
Storm-bound, shipwrecked and cast-away,

By horrid fate compelled to stay,
They yielded not to grim despair,
But bearded Winter in his lair;
Bravely building their snow house domes,
They settled into northern homes.
Lost to their ken is old Norway,
But cherished still in their memory.
The rising sun began the year;
Four months his rays shone full and clear;
A month he gave a milder light,
'Twixt the long day and longer night.
For half the year Aurora's beams,
The moon's soft ray, and starry gleams,
Guided the hunter to his home,
Whene'er he chose afar to roam.
Foremost among his tribe and clan,
There lived a hardy little man;
His wife, renowned for spirit high,
Rejoiced in her large family;—
Four sturdy sons, four maidens brown,
Gathered in harmony around
Their fireplace, and together dwelt,
And love for one another felt.
One fateful day there came along
Six Iceland fishers, stern and strong.
The Esquimaux in terror fled
From spirits evil, so they said;
But meeting them with friendly mien,
The pigmies soon at ease were seen.
The giants more contented grew,

And eager searched for knowledge new;
But erst they thought of native shore,
And longed to view their home once more.
At length, in venturous spirit bold,
Their purpose to their friends they told,
To seek their lov'd land once again,
By crossing on the frozen main.
The trial made, the deed was done!
A victory great, and nobly won!
Three families assistance lent.
Upon returning they were bent,
Till finding this a better land,
They settled on the barren strand;
In mission schools were kindly taught,
And daily grew in word and thought.

Five years rolled by; consumption's claim
Was laid upon the mother's frame.
The father loved his youngest child,
And with her crossed the ocean wild;
With many mishaps, much fatigue,
They found a home in Winnipeg.

Five years again had claimed their own;
The daughter now to woman grown,
Though but a little child for size,
Assayed a wond'rous enterprise—
To win from gen'rous strangers' hand,
By telling of her native land,
Her fortune, and to meet once more

Her sisters three and brothers four.
Pray tell me, friend, didst e'er thou find
A braver spirit, nobler mind,
A name more worthy to go down
On hist'ry's page with bright renown?

Captain Holm recently returned to Copenhagen, after having spent two years and a half exploring the almost unknown region of the east coast of Greenland. Although ten or twelve expeditions have set out for East Greenland in the past two centuries, almost all of them in search of the lost Norsemen, who were supposed to have settled there, only one ship ever reached the coast.

The great ice masses, sometimes hundreds of miles wide, that are perpetually piled up against the shore, have kept explorers from East Greenland long after all Arctic lands were fairly well known. With three assistants, Captain Holm landed at Cape Farewell, and then went north some four hundred miles. He has returned with large collections, representing the flora, fauna, geology, and anthropology of this hitherto unknown portion of the earth's surface. He found in those cold and dismal regions, isolated from the world, a race of people who had never heard, or known, of the great civilized nations of the earth. They seemed to lead happy lives, and live in a communicative way in hamlets. They differ entirely in language, and physical character, from the Esquimaux of West Greenland.—*Demorest's Monthly.*